Grumpy Bear

Best Friend Bear

Secret Bear

This book belongs to:
_____

Wish Bear

Love-a-lot Bear

Published by Scholastic Inc.
90 Old Sherman Turnpike, Danbury, CT 06816.

SCHOLASTIC and associated logos are trademarks and/or registered trademarks of Scholastic Inc.

ISBN 0-439-83579-8

First Scholastic Printing, February 2006

Care Bears Friendship Club
Wishful Thinking

by
Quinlan B. Lee

Illustrated by
Warner McGee

SCHOLASTIC INC.

New York   Toronto   London   Auckland   Sydney
Mexico City   New Delhi   Hong Kong   Buenos Aires

One lazy afternoon, as the Care Bears were watching the clouds drift by, Secret Bear picked a dandelion.

"Make a wish," said Wish Bear.

"What did you wish for?" Best Friend Bear asked.

"Is it a secret?"

"Oh no," Secret Bear replied.
"Not every wish is a secret."

"I wished Care-a-lot had a park where we could play all day and **do all of our favorite things.**"

"Oh, I wish that, too!"

said Cheer Bear. She quickly picked
another dandelion and blew it. She added,
"I wish for a park with rainbow slides
and a jungle gym and seesaws and . . ."

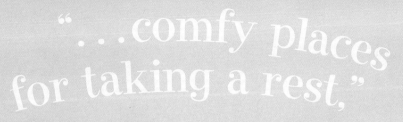

"...comfy places for taking a rest,"

finished Bedtime Bear, smiling.

Just then some other Care Bears skated up
to say hello to their friends. They spotted the dandelions,
and they were soon making wishes, too.

"You know what would be fun?" asked Funshine Bear. "I wish there was a place where we could do tricks on our skates, like twirl around and flip upside down.

"Upside down?!?" cried Grumpy Bear. "Of course," Funshine Bear replied. "It's the perfect way to turn a frown into a smile."

Love-a-lot Bear leaned back on her cloud.
"There's one thing I would love a lot," she said.

"I wish for a place where . . .

. we could all go fishing."

Bashful Heart Bear was listening
quietly to his friends talk.

"What do you wish for?" Wish Bear
asked him.

"Baseball,"

Bashful Heart Bear said softly.
"I love baseball. I wish there was
a place where we could all play
anytime we wanted."

"I wish for a big table where we could all share snacks and lemonade after the game," said Share Bear.

"That would make the park perfect."

The Care Bears sat dreaming
for a while.

"Well...,"

Wish Bear finally said.

"Well, what?"
asked Cheer Bear.

"Well, what about the park?"
Wish Bear replied.

Grumpy Bear sighed. "It was only wishful thinking," he said sadly.

"Only wishful thinking?"

Wish Bear exclaimed. "There's no such thing! We have everything we need to make our wishes come true!"

"We do?"
Grumpy Bear asked.

"Sure," said Wish Bear. "Look around! There are lots of rainbows for sliding. And we could get some bars for these stars and make a jungle gym in no time."

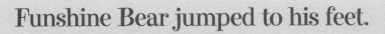

Funshine Bear jumped to his feet.

"**You're right!**

With a little work, those clouds
over there would make a
great place to skate."

"I could share some things I have at Care-a-lot Castle," said Share Bear. "We could use them to make a table, some seesaws, and maybe even some baseball bats."

"What are we waiting for?"
Wish Bear asked.

"Let's go!"

The Care Bears hurried to Care-a-lot Castle
to get everything they needed to build the park.

Soon the Care Bears were working together
to build their dream park.

"This will be a great spot for *fishin'*,"
said Love-a-lot Bear.

"Are you sure you don't mean *wishin'?"* asked Wish Bear, giggling.

With a little teamwork, the park
was finished and ready for fun.

The Care Bears spent many happy hours playing and doing all of their favorite things.

"This is perfect," said Share Bear. "Thanks for making our wishes come true, Wish Bear."

"It wasn't just me," Wish Bear replied.
"It was all of us."

"When we work together, we can make all of our wishes come true," she said.

Grumpy Bear winked. "And that isn't **wishful thinking,"** he added.

Can You Make Wishes Come True Like Wish Bear?

Everyone has wishes and dreams,
just like the Care Bears.

♥ What do you wish for?

The Care Bears learned
that sometimes it takes
work to make a wish
come true.

♥ Did you ever have
to do something to
make a wish come true?

♥ What did you do?

♥ Was it hard?

The Care Bears were able to build their dream park
because they worked together.
- ♥ Have you worked with your friends
  to build something?
- ♥ How did you work together?
- ♥ How did you feel when you were finished?

Bashful Heart Bear

Cheer Bear

Share Bear

Bedtime Bear

Funshine Bear